leapfrog
Rhyme
Time

The Lonely Pirate

by Jillian Powell

Illustrated by Anna C. Leplar

W
FRANKLIN WATTS
LONDON•SYDNEY

leapfrog

Rhyme
Time

The Lonely
Pirate

First published in 2007 by
Franklin Watts
338 Euston Road
London
NW1 3BH

Franklin Watts Australia
Level 17/207 Kent Street
Sydney
NSW 2000

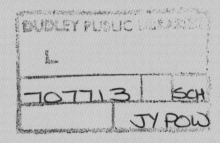

Text © Jillian Powell 2007
Illustration © Anna C. Leplar 2007

A CIP catalogue record for this book is available
from the British Library.

ISBN 978 0 7496 7101 3 (hbk)
ISBN 978 0 7496 7793 0 (pbk)

Series Editor: Jackie Hamley
Series Advisor: Dr Barrie Wade
Series Designer: Peter Scoulding

Printed in China

Franklin Watts is a division of
Hachette Children's Books
an Hachette Livre UK company.

There was once
a lonely pirate.

He had no friends at sea.

He flew the Jolly Roger,
but no one was there
to see.

It's easy to get lonely
when there's nobody
in sight –

just the blue sea
and the blue sky ...

... and the moon and stars at night.

Sometimes he played
the fiddle,

but he made an awful din.

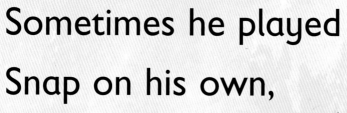

Sometimes he played
Snap on his own,

but then he'd always win.

Sometimes he climbed
the ship's mast,

to look for another boat.

Or he'd hook things
on his fishing rod,

to see if they would float!

He tried calling
to the seagulls,
but they flew
the other way.

He tried singing
to the whales,

22

but he just scared
them away!

Then one day
he found an island,

with trees round
a mountain peak.

In the trees, he saw
a parrot with a red
and yellow beak.

He soon stopped being
lonely once he heard
the parrot squawk.

For he took that parrot
with him ...

... and he taught
it how to talk!

31

Leapfrog has been specially designed to fit the requirements of the National Literacy Strategy. It offers real books for beginning readers by top authors and illustrators. There are 67 Leapfrog stories to choose from:

* hardback